B-135
.99¢

D1520120

Travel Safety

Perspectives on Violence

by Gus Gedatus

Consultant:
Vikki L. Sanders
Workplace Violence Prevention Coordinator
Department of Labor and Industry/
Workplace Safety Consultation
St. Paul, Minnesota

LifeMatters
an imprint of Capstone Press
Mankato, Minnesota

LifeMatters Books are published by Capstone Press
PO Box 669 • 151 Good Counsel Drive • Mankato, Minnesota 56002
http://www.capstone-press.com

Printed in the United States of America

Library of Congress Cataloging-in-Publication Data
Gedatus, Gustav Mark.
    Travel safety / by Gus Gedatus.
        p.   cm. — (Perspectives on violence)
    Includes bibliographical references and index.
    Summary: Discusses ways to remain safe while traveling, covering such topics as unexpected situations, weather, public transportation, money matters, and foreign travel.
    ISBN 0-7368-0426-9 (book) — ISBN 0-7368-0439-0 (series)
    1. Travel—Safety measures—Juvenile literature. [1. Travel—Safety measures. 2. Safety.] I. Title. II. Series
    G151.G44 2000
    910´.2´02—dc21   99-058932
                                                          CIP

Staff Credits
Rebecca Aldridge, Charles Pederson, editors; Adam Lazar, designer; Jody Theisen, photo researcher

Photo Credits
Cover: PNI/©Jeff Greenberg, large; ©Alexander Talaras, small
International Stock/©Peter Langone, 10; ©Don Romero, 14; ©Tony Demin, 16; ©Giovanni Lunardi, 24; ©Jay Thomas, 27; ©Ron Frehm, 43; ©George Ancona, 47; ©Tom O'Brien, 48; ©Don Romero, 54
Transparencies, Inc./© J. Faircloth, 7; ©Dick Young, 8; ©Jim McGuire, 22; ©Novastock/Gerard Fritz, 37
Unicorn/41; ©Jim Shippee, 35
Uniphoto/©Raintree Media, 51; ©David M. Doody, 56

A 0 9 8 7 6 5 4 3 2 1

Table of Contents

Chapter Overview

Traveling offers many different, exciting opportunities. Certain safety procedures can make travel more carefree. An important part of travel safety is always remaining aware of your surroundings.

Traveling with another person or in a group is a good idea.

Concern for safety is important, even when traveling to or through familiar places.

When talking with others, it is a good idea to set physical and emotional boundaries.

Chapter 1

Remaining Safe Away From Home

Travel offers many chances for exciting experiences. It can broaden your horizons and make life richer. For example, it may allow you to meet relatives you have never seen before. You may meet people in cultures different from your own. You may develop new interests in art, history, nature, or other areas. You may have adventures that make you feel like an explorer. You might find that the more you travel, the more you want to travel again.

"We will travel as far as we can, but we cannot in one lifetime see all that we would like to see or to learn all that we hunger to know."—Loren Eiseley

This book describes many different travel situations. It presents steps for remaining safe and healthy while traveling. Once you get used to taking certain safety precautions, they will become good travel habits. Then you can travel and have fun with fewer worries.

Typically, travelers get caught up with details. A flight may be delayed, or an airline may move a plane's departure from one gate to another. Detours around construction may occur. Because of a misunderstanding, friends who have agreed to meet may end up at separate places. Many things are beyond a person's control. Surprises and changes may alter a trip, but they don't need to make it a bad experience.

Getting Ready to Go

You can make your trip safer and, at the same time, easier. By preparing for travel, you can focus on having a good time while still being aware of your surroundings. Awareness means taking as much control as possible over your well-being. It doesn't mean becoming afraid.

If you have already visited your destination, think about what happened. List things that you want to do differently on this trip. If you are going somewhere new, read about the place before you leave. Maps of your destination can help you plan your exploration routes in advance. Talk with people who have been to these places. These people may point out places to go or places to avoid. Lots of information is available at your local public library and on the Internet.

Adventurous but Not Careless

Traveling away from home often makes people want to have adventures. That's one reason why people travel. If you want an adventure, by all means try new and different things as you travel. You may have heard the saying, "When in Rome, do as the Romans do." That means if you want to fit in, follow the customs of the local people. However, that doesn't mean you should do something without thinking. It doesn't mean you have to eat or drink foods that may be unsafe.

It is not difficult to remain safe if you travel alone. However, traveling with another person or a group can add to the fun and is safer. Friends can watch out for one another. It's important to be aware of what is going on around you, even while you have fun.

Remembering Safe Travel in Familiar Places

When people travel in unfamiliar places, safety is likely to be a major concern. Even after you learn about a new place, it can be filled with unknown things. However, when you visit or pass through a familiar area often, you may become careless. This may be the case with your neighborhood, your hometown, or a city you visit frequently.

Sometimes cities and even neighborhoods change. Areas that were once safe may no longer be safe. For example, crime or poor roads may make areas unsafe. This kind of change is another reason why it's important to consider your surroundings. Whether you are walking, biking, driving, or waiting for public transportation, it's always a good idea to look around. Even the most familiar places may have changed.

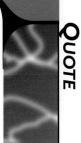
"Do not leave your common sense at home. You are more vulnerable when you are in unfamiliar surroundings."—American Automobile Association

VANESSA, AGE 17

Vanessa found her seat on the train. A man named Mr. Barnes, who was about her father's age, sat down next to her. Almost immediately he started to chat with her. Vanessa enjoyed his conversation. After a while, Mr. Barnes started touching Vanessa's arm or shoulder as he talked. Once, when she got up for a magazine, he touched her lower back as she passed him. Vanessa was very uncomfortable.

"I don't want to offend you," she explained kindly but firmly. "But I am not comfortable when people I have just met touch me. I like talking with you, but please don't touch me." The man apologized. For the rest of the trip, Vanessa and Mr. Barnes kept talking, but he didn't touch her again.

Strangers and Boundaries

Without a doubt, much of the fun in traveling comes from meeting people. You might meet someone while waiting in a line. A stranger may help you when you are struggling with language in a foreign country. You can marvel at how different yet how similar people from other places can be.

Yet, when dealing with others, most people have boundaries. Especially in dealing with strangers, however, it is important to know what your boundaries are. These are physical or emotional limits that keep us feeling comfortable. A physical boundary is the space you keep between yourself and another person while talking. You may need more distance with strangers than with close friends.

Most North Americans are comfortable keeping strangers at about an arm's length away. This is not true of people from every culture. In some cultures, people may almost touch when speaking together. If a stranger gets too close to you or touches you, your boundaries may be challenged. Only you can decide what feels right in a situation.

Boundaries include not only your physical space but also information about you. You must decide how much information to give out. People usually ask questions because they are interested in you. However, a few people may be looking for someone to victimize, or make a victim, in some way.

Many experts believe that teens are more likely than adults to have their boundaries tested. Teens sometimes have weaker boundaries than adults. This is because teens have less experience enforcing their boundaries. They may believe that enforcing their boundaries seems rude. Like all people, teens should know their boundaries and be prepared to enforce them. To keep themselves safe, this is necessary no matter what someone might think of them.

If any situation does not feel right, trust your instincts. Step back if someone is too close. Don't give out personal information about yourself. Don't worry about hurting someone's feelings. You need to take care of yourself first. Worry about someone else's feelings only after you feel safe.

Points to Consider

Why do you think being aware of your surroundings is important?

How could you get into trouble traveling, even in a place that is familiar to you?

How can you determine what your boundaries are?

Chapter
Overview

It's a good idea to listen to your instincts in judging if a situation is safe.

Walking or running confidently is important to safety. Watching out for others when skating, biking, or driving is important, too.

Some everyday medications and supplies may not be readily available everywhere.

Your physical safety is more important than your belongings. Stay calm and hand over whatever a robber asks.

The American or Canadian embassy in your destination country can help in an emergency.

Chapter 2

Personal Travel Safety

Most people travel every day. Much of this travel is done on foot or on wheels, with muscle power. As you walk, run, skate, or bike, it's a good idea to do it defensively. You need to protect yourself because people often are busy and preoccupied with their own movements. You need to be alert for your own safety.

Walking and Running

You may walk a lot when you travel at home or away from home. No matter how you get around, always carry identification. This will help if you should have an accident. As you walk, always consider the area and people around you. Listen to your instincts. They can help you remain in control of your safety.

Sarah and Kasi were jogging around the lake. They noticed a **SARAH AND KASI, AGE 16** woman in a gray pickup truck pass them several times. They thought they could see her looking at them from her side-view mirror. Not many other people were out. The girls picked up their speed slightly. They were concerned but did not want to appear scared. When they reached the hot dog stand, they stopped to get a juice and talk with the seller. The woman in the truck saw Sarah and Kasi talking with the hot dog seller. She didn't drive by anymore after that.

If you walk or run in a busy area, keep your eyes open. Drivers, bicyclists, skaters, and other runners may be wrapped up in their own activities. Use well-lit public places where lots of people are. If signs are posted to direct foot, bike, or skate traffic, obey them. If an area is known for crime or for fast or careless driving, consider a different route. Run with at least one partner when possible. This is particularly true for females, especially if it is getting dark or if any of the route is dangerous.

The most severe injuries in biking and skating accidents are to the head. Wear a helmet while biking or skating. You will be less likely to have a serious or fatal injury in an accident.

If you have to go through an area that feels unsafe, walk or run confidently. Move as though you know where you are going and can take care of yourself. This positive nonverbal attitude helps you to look like a strong person, not like a victim. If you get lost or need help, stop to ask for assistance in a public place. For example, stop at a store, restaurant, post office, or library. You also could stop at the reception desk of a nearby office, hotel, or other business.

Skating

In-line skating or roller skating is good exercise. When choosing a course to skate, consider the following safety tips. These apply whether at home or in a foreign country.

Keep out of the path of motor vehicles. Watch out for drivers' sudden movements. Also watch for people in parked cars opening their doors. Choose routes that aren't too busy.

Be aware of other skaters, bikers, and pedestrians, or people on foot. You may know where you are headed, but other people might not notice you.

Choose roads or paved paths that are in good shape. Ruts, ridges, sand, or gaps in the pavement can cause nasty falls. These poor conditions may force skaters into the path of motor vehicles.

Wear a helmet and knee, wrist, and shoulder pads. This safety equipment reduces the likelihood of injury if you fall or run into something.

Biking

All over the world, bikes are a popular way to get around. When riding a bike, consider these safety tips:

You may need to enter or cross a road from an alley or side street. Always stop and look left, then right, then left again in such situations. Many accidents occur in midblock because drivers aren't prepared for someone on a bike or skates to appear.

Ride in the same direction as motorized traffic. Riding with traffic is much safer for bicyclists. Drivers know better what to expect.

Avoid riding at night. This is especially true in places with narrow roads or where speed limits exceed 35 miles (60 kilometers) per hour. If you must ride at night, use reflectors and lights and wear light-colored clothing.

When turning, watch the path of vehicles around you and how close they are to you. Always look behind you before turning.

Obey all traffic signs and laws. Learn the local laws in unfamiliar places.

At busy intersections, walk your bike across the road.

Medicines for Minor Pain

Physical activity that you are not used to, such as lots of walking or biking, can cause temporary pain. To deal with these aches, you may want to bring your own supply of pain relievers. Diarrhea medicine, antacids, and cold pills are other medicines that are good to have on hand. Diarrhea medicine helps when normally solid human waste becomes runny and frequent. Antacids fight acid in the stomach. Bandages, eyewash, lotions, and for some destinations, bug repellants also may be important for your comfort.

These products usually are easy to find at your hometown drugstore. However, they may not be readily available in all foreign countries or on certain trips. For example, they may be hard to find if needed while on a bike trip in the woods.

Staying Calm and Dealing With Trouble

It is important to remember that your physical safety is more important than your belongings. When traveling, you are not likely to be robbed or assaulted. You can lessen the chance of an emergency by remaining aware of where you are and who is nearby. However, sometimes such crimes do happen, even if a traveler is being cautious. For instance, in a crowded place, a thief might steal your purse or backpack without being noticed. If someone tries to rob you, calmly hand over whatever the person demands.

For information on English-speaking doctors in other countries, you can contact The International Association for Medical Assistance to Travelers, 417 Center Street, New York, NY 14902.

If you must run from danger, you need to know where it is safe to go. This is another reason to be aware of your surroundings. If you are in danger of assault, don't panic. Get away from the situation as soon as possible. If you can't, use clear and direct words, eye contact, and strong body language. Make a scene to attract attention. Physically fight back only as a last resort. People who fight back during an assault are more likely to be injured than people who don't.

Who to Ask for Help

If you are a victim of crime, contact the local police. In most North American cities, do whatever you would do at home. However, in foreign countries you may have difficulty. Local laws may confuse you, or language might be a barrier. If so, the Regional Security Officer Consular/Consumer Section of the American or Canadian embassy may be helpful. You can contact the one in your destination country. An ambassador who represents your home country works at the embassy with staff members.

If you are accused of a crime, the embassy also is your best contact. Embassies in foreign countries are meant to protect their citizens who travel there.

"By the time I took my trip I felt like I had become buddies with Rico, our travel agent. He gave me some great tips that made my time in Buenos Aires a lot of fun!"—Bernard, age 15

You or a traveling companion may have a serious health concern. If so, you may need information about hospitals and clinics. Also, there are more than 3,000 English-speaking, Western-trained doctors in 140 different countries.

Points to Consider

Why do you think walking or running confidently is important?

How could you learn about biking rules in another country?

How would you react if someone tried to rob you?

Chapter
Overview

There are many ways to be safe while in a car.

Being careful in dealing with your money on public transportation is important.

It's a good idea to keep an eye on valuables while using a public phone or restroom.

Listening to weather warnings is important. So is knowing where you are going before you leave.

Chapter 3

Safety in Motor Vehicles and on Public Transportation

Driving a Car

Now or in the future you may use a car for your primary transportation. Whether you drive near your own home or in an unfamiliar place, consider these safety ideas.

Keep your car in good mechanical condition to avoid breakdowns. A car in good condition is safer in bad weather or in emergencies.

Fill the gas tank during daylight hours. More service stations are open, and criminal activity is less likely.

Always lock expensive items such as cameras in the trunk.

Get a cell phone if you can. A cell phone is helpful especially if you have an emergency in an isolated area.

Hold your keys in your hand as you approach your car. Don't wait until you get to your car to look for them.

Check the backseat before getting into the car, even if the doors have been locked. This will keep you from being surprised by an intruder hiding there.

Never pick up hitchhikers.

Honk the horn to get other people's attention if you are in danger while parked or moving.

If you are in a hotel, ask the desk clerk about areas of town to avoid. The clerk also may know special precautions to take while driving a rental car.

For driving in areas with cold winters, keep emergency items in the trunk. These can include a mat that has traction, or gripping power, a small shovel, and a bag of sand. Flares, blankets, and a flashlight also might be useful. Food such as candy bars can provide energy if you are stuck for a long time.

You may get a flat tire in a dangerous or dark location. If so, drive slowly to the nearest busy public place. Do not change the tire in the dangerous location.

Another car may bump you from behind or someone may say something is wrong with your car. Don't pull over in either of these situations. Drive to a gas station or a busy, well-lit place and call for help.

Don't pull over for flashing headlights. The lights on emergency vehicles usually are on top. They usually are red, yellow, or blue.

If you plan to rent a car, find out if the rental company marks its cars. It is better not to have a car marked with a rental agency sticker. You will be less noticeable to a thief or criminal who targets travelers.

Be polite to other drivers. Today's crowded streets and freeways may lead drivers to aggressive behavior called road rage. People who drive cooperatively are likely to receive cooperation from other drivers in return.

Last July while traveling through Europe, Darrell saw someone **DARRELL, AGE 18** steal a man's duffel bag. The victim was buying a subway token. He set his bag down on the ground to get some money from his wallet. Out of nowhere, a guy grabbed the bag, hopped over the turnstile, and ran off. The victim shouted, but the thief disappeared into the crowd.

Public Transportation

People all over the world rely on public transportation. They may use subways, buses, trains, or streetcars to get to school or work. Using public transportation is usually safe and predictable. However, basic safety considerations still apply.

When paying for tokens or passes, have the correct change in your hand. Ticket booths are often busy. Someone may be watching to see what your wallet contains. By keeping your valuables in a purse, pack, or bag, a thief is less likely to steal from you. However, a thief sometimes steals an entire bag. A better solution is to carry valuables in a pocket or fanny pack with a zipper. If you use a fanny pack, keep it on the front of your body.

Busy areas are common ground for pickpockets. A child or even a woman with a baby can be a pickpocket. Often these people work with someone. This accomplice may try to distract the victim by:

Jostling

Asking for directions or the time

Pointing out a spill on clothing

Creating a disturbance

Buses and streetcars are generally safer than trains. Buses and streetcars move aboveground. On buses, the driver usually can see activity on board. Police are more likely to be nearby. However, if you are on a crowded bus or streetcar, be especially aware of people around you. A thief can easily steal a purse, bag, or package and disappear into the crowd. He or she may be long gone before you realize that something of yours is missing.

To reach trains and subways, riders often must walk down stairs and wait on large underground platforms. During daytime hours, these places are often crowded. It is a good habit to use trains at times like this. At night, waiting for a train may be different. You may be one of only a few people waiting. If you have a choice of platforms or stops, wait somewhere that is well lit and well populated. Some locations may even have security people or cameras. These measures help discourage crime.

Many major subway and train systems have an increasing number of security people near ticket booths and on platforms. This has resulted in fewer incidents of theft and mugging. The presence of security people also prevents most destruction of property.

Safely deboarding, or getting off, a bus or train at night can be a challenge. As you exit, follow the crowd. People who lag behind may be chosen as targets for theft or assault. Likewise, if you feel uncomfortable about a group of people at your approaching stop, trust that instinct. Stay on the bus. Walking a few extra blocks from a different stop might be a bother, but it could be safer.

Public Restrooms and Telephones

When using public restrooms, be careful with your valuables. Do not place them on the floor of a toilet stall. If possible, hold them on your lap. Another option is to hang them around your neck. Hanging them on the hook of the stall door is also a good option. However, many hooks are high on the door, and thieves can easily reach them from outside the stall. If you travel with other people, leave bags with each other and take turns using the restroom.

If you need to use a public telephone, find one in a busy place. Keep an eye on the area around you. This can be a challenge when you are occupied in conversation, but it is important. Place any bags behind you, either away from the door or between you and a wall. In a phone booth, face the door while talking.

Local Traffic and Weather Warnings

All of the planning in the world can't prevent sudden travel changes. Road construction, traffic jams, or severe weather could alter a route or lengthen travel time. If you're in an English-speaking place, read the daily newspaper or watch local television news broadcasts. In Canada, you may call Travel Canada for traffic updates. In the United States, you can contact the American Automobile Association (AAA). Look in the section on Useful Addresses and Internet Sites on page 62. It has contact information for these and other helpful organizations.

If you are staying in a hotel, explain to the desk clerk where you plan to go. Ask if the clerk knows of any recent obstacle to your safe travel. If you are in a non-English-speaking country, ask a tour guide. As a last resort, local people who speak English may be helpful.

Reading Maps and Getting Directions

Knowing about your destination before you travel can save you trouble. It decreases the likelihood of becoming lost. Many excellent map books are available at libraries or bookstores. It is a good idea to have one map for an entire state or country. It is ideal to bring a set of maps for wherever you want to go in an unfamiliar place.

Several Internet sites offer helpful map services that are free. These Internet sites give easy-to-follow instructions. Usually they require a starting place and a destination. The site provides written directions or a map that can make your trip safer and easier. Check your local library if you don't have Internet access at home or school.

People often hear about interesting attractions while they are traveling. Before taking an unplanned side trip, locate the destination on a map while still in your hotel room. Then, if you are unclear about directions, you can ask the hotel desk clerk for help. Also, pulling out a map in public makes you look like a tourist. This increases the chance of being a victim of someone who targets tourists. You also could try a local chamber of commerce, tourism office, or local police station for help. As a last resort, ask people in public places.

Points to Consider

How would you react if you thought someone on a crowded bus was trying to steal something from you?

What is the safest way to handle your cash while paying for a bus or subway pass?

In your opinion, what are the three most important safety tips for driving a car?

Let's say you have a friend who is going to travel to an unfamiliar big city. Your friend is afraid of getting lost. What advice would you give him or her?

Chapter Overview

It's important not to travel with jewelry or other items that may be difficult to replace if lost or stolen.

Personalizing your luggage helps you keep track of it better.

It's a good idea to keep money and other valuables next to your body, not in a purse or bag.

Traveler's checks are a good idea because they can be replaced if lost or stolen. Credit cards and ATMs help you avoid having to carry lots of cash.

Always keeping your bags with you in a travel hub is important.

Chapter 4

Long-Distance Travel

Long-distance travel, whether to another state or another country, changes your routine. You have to bring fewer of the clothing and personal items you need for everyday use. You probably handle more money than usual. You sleep in a different place and are surrounded by strangers. Careful planning and ongoing alertness can make long-distance travel more enjoyable.

DID YOU KNOW?

Some people use suitcase alarms. If someone attempts to steal or interfere with the luggage, the alarm goes off.

Luggage

Most experienced travelers advise packing light. The fewer bags you have, the easier it is to get around. You can keep track of them more easily. You are less likely to have something stolen. It is important not to pack valuables in your luggage. Don't take valuables such as jewelry that cannot be replaced. Keep cash, tickets, and passport in a money belt under your clothes. That way, if your luggage is lost or stolen, you still have these important items.

It's best not to let a stranger carry your luggage for you. The person could steal your bag or attempt to hide an illegal item in it. If your bags are heavy, plan ahead and get a rack with wheels for them.

Sometimes a suitcase disappears because another traveler mistakes it for his or her own. Personalizing your luggage with a sticker or bright piece of ribbon can help to avoid this. If your luggage is a popular color or style, personalizing it is particularly wise. If you lose track of your bags, personalization can help you recognize them.

Another good idea is to include a note with your name, address, and telephone number inside each piece of luggage. On the outside of your luggage use covered tags. This way your personal information is not easily seen.

"My grandpa gave me a tough, grungy old suitcase that he used in the 1950s. It holds a lot. It'll never break open. No one would ever want to steal it. Plus, it looks cool."—Mark, age 16

If an airline loses your bags, contact its customer service department. Usually, the luggage is found and is brought to your hotel or home free of charge. If the luggage cannot be found, the U.S. government requires the airline to pay for losses up to $1,250 per passenger. The requirement applies to checked luggage only. Most airlines do not pay for lost cash, cameras, jewelry, or other items you carry directly onto the plane.

Money and Valuables

Many safety experts recommend that travelers carry money in at least two places. Carry cash for expenses such as snacks or cab fare in a front pocket or wallet. Keep larger sums of money, credit cards, and other valuables out of sight. You can wear a money belt under your clothes for that purpose. If you are robbed, give up the wallet or the money in your pocket. Most of your funds and other valuables remain safely in the money belt. If you travel with your family or a group, split up cash among members. That way, if one person is robbed, the others still have some cash.

When you make a more expensive purchase, try not to display too much cash. People may be watching for travelers who have lots of money with them. Be aware of suspicious people. This is particularly important when you are using cash or credit cards.

The Federal Express World Business and Calendar Advisor has phone numbers for U.S. Chambers of Commerce worldwide. Call 1-800-247-4747.

Traveler's Checks

Traveler's checks that banks issue are an alternative to cash. If the checks are lost or stolen, they can be replaced easily without cost to you. Travel experts recommend keeping a list of the serial numbers of the checks in a separate place from the checks. Also, it is a good idea to leave a list of serial numbers with someone back home. If the checks are lost, having those numbers makes the replacement process easier.

Credit Cards

Like traveler's checks, credit cards help travelers avoid the need to carry much cash. In an emergency, credit cards can be used to get money quickly. Before traveling, find out how much cash your credit card can provide if you need emergency funds. Bring only the necessary number of credit cards.

CHARLENE, AGE 18

Charlene put her credit card into an automatic teller machine (ATM) in France. A young man rode up on a motorcycle to use the ATM. He said his name was Claude and began chatting with Charlene about her trip. As he talked, Charlene noticed that he was moving toward the ATM. Suddenly, he reached for the slot where Charlene's card would come out. As he did, Charlene screamed "Police" at the top of her lungs. Startled, Claude sped off on his motorcycle. A second later Charlene's card slid out of the ATM. She was glad that Claude's conversation had not kept her from staying alert.

Automatic Teller Machines

Automatic teller machines (ATMs) can make travel safer. It is not always necessary for travelers to bring much cash from home. Cash is available from ATMs in most major cities of the world. Just make sure that your destination has ATMs that will accept your particular cash card or credit card. Your bank or credit card company usually can provide this information. Otherwise, call the U.S. Chamber of Commerce Office in your destination country.

Airports and Bus and Train Stations

Travel hubs such as airports or bus and train stations are becoming more crowded all the time. Criminals may look for victims among the crowd in these centers of activity. In some cities, travel hubs are areas for crime. Such crimes as drug activity or participating in sexual acts for money may occur in these places. Teens who look lost, tired, or unhappy may be likely targets for some criminals. It's important to remember that having clear boundaries reduces the chance of becoming a crime victim.

One good rule in travel hubs is never to agree to carry parcels or baggage for strangers. No matter how friendly or harmless people appear, you can never be sure what their parcel may contain. You could get into serious legal trouble if the package contains an illegal item.

The most common places for people to be robbed are bus and train stations, airports, and crowded streets.

It is possible that something you wear or carry may set off the alarm at an airport X-ray machine. If you are stopped for a security check, first get your bags from the machine. If security workers do unexpected checks, a traveler's bags may be stolen.

It is important to deal seriously with airport security or customs officials. Joking about safety may amuse your friends. However, such comments can get you into trouble. For example, a security officer may hear someone joke about a bomb in his or her bag. The officer will likely arrest that person and question him or her.

Flying

Flying is a comfortable and quick way to get from place to place. You can do several things to make flying safer. For example, avoid carrying large items onto a plane. If you must store a bag far away from your seat, you risk having the bag stolen. In a crowded airplane, you may not notice someone walking off with your bag.

Listen to the in-flight safety briefing the flight attendants give.
Review the information on the safety card provided. Follow
directions about the use of electronic devices because they can
interfere with a plane's communication system. Locate the two
exits nearest your seat. Keep your seatbelt securely fastened when
you are seated. Keep it fastened even when the "fasten seatbelt"
sign is turned off. If you have any other safety questions, ask a
flight attendant.

Points to Consider

What items would you pack for a two-week trip to Egypt?

What would you do if you lost a suitcase at the airport?

How would you respond to someone who started a
conversation with you while you were using an ATM?

Chapter Overview

Chapter
Overview

Finding out about a hotel's security before you reserve a room is a good idea.

It's best to keep valuables with you or store them in the hotel safe.

It's important to keep doors locked and question unexpected visitors before letting them in.

You need to familiarize yourself with safety measures in case of fire.

Chapter 5

Hotel Safety

When traveling away from home, many people stay at hotels. Before reserving a room, it is a good idea to get answers to your questions about hotel security. The hotel, a travel agent, or a guidebook may be able to help you answer questions such as:

Do all room doors have dead bolt locks? This is a very strong and secure type of lock.

Are keys or electronic vinyl cards used to unlock the door? Experts consider electronic cards safer because codes change with each new set of guests.

Does the hotel offer a safe or safety-deposit box?

Valuable items should be stored in the hotel safe. Many insurance companies do not pay for lost items that aren't stored.

Is there off-street car parking for hotel guests? Is the parking lot or ramp well lit?

Is public transportation to the hotel available?

Is the area around the hotel safe?

Most hotels offer the best in safety for their guests. Be careful with your belongings and use all available security measures. That way, you are less likely to be a victim of crime. There are many ways to make your stay safer.

Storing Valuables

Don't leave valuables in your room when you are out. Carry them with you or place them in a hotel safe. Many hotels provide a safe-deposit box free of charge. It is not likely that anyone could break into your room. However, you may have trouble getting the hotel to replace anything that is stolen from your room. Ask the front desk clerk about getting a safe-deposit box.

Keeping Your Room Secure

It is important to stay safe while in your hotel room. Use all locks provided when you are in your room. Make sure all doors are locked, including balcony doors and doors to neighboring rooms. If someone comes to your door claiming to be a hotel employee, ask for identification. Call the hotel desk to ask if they sent someone to your door. Don't open the door for other strangers.

Jerry wasn't expecting anyone, but someone was knocking on his

JERRY, AGE 17

hotel room door. Jerry looked through the peephole. He saw a man standing next to a cart with a dinner tray on it. Jerry asked through the door, "Can I help you?"

The man replied, "Room service, sir."

"I didn't order anything. Hold on, please," Jerry said.

Jerry called down to the kitchen. He and the woman taking orders there figured out what had happened. Someone in the room two doors down from Jerry had placed the order. The woman simply wrote down the wrong room number.

Jerry went back and opened the door. "Helen wrote down the wrong number. You're supposed to take that to room 472."

"Sorry, sir," said the man.

"No problem," said Jerry.

Travel experts say that the safest hotel rooms are from the second to the seventh floors above ground level. People with criminal intentions who enter from the outside can't get in easily. Yet these rooms are low enough for fire equipment to reach.

Preparing for Fire and Other Emergencies

It is unlikely that there will be an emergency in your hotel. However, if you are prepared for an emergency, you are less likely to panic. As soon as you arrive at your room, read any safety information. It is usually posted on the inside of the door to your room. Locate the nearest fire exit. Consider how to find this exit in the dark. For example, count the number of doors between your room and the fire stairs.

If you suspect that there is a fire in your hotel, call the hotel operator immediately. Then follow these steps:

Do not open the door if the doorknob feels warm.

If the door feels cool, open it while on your knees. Close the door quickly if smoke comes in. If there is no smoke, close the door behind you and take the room key.

Crawl along the floor, where there is more oxygen, to the nearest fire exit. Walk quickly but carefully down the stairs.

Avoid the elevator. You could get trapped in it if the electricity goes off.

If you cannot leave your room, don't jump from the window. Instead, hang a bedsheet out the window to get the attention of rescuers. If the window is permanently locked, break it with a heavy object from the room.

Fill the bathtub with water. Place a wet towel over the base of your room door. This will keep smoke from entering the room.

If smoke enters the room, tie a wet towel over your mouth and nose to filter the air. Crack the window at the top or bottom to draw smoke out of the room.

Points to Consider

What do you think are the three most important safety considerations when staying in a hotel?

Where would you keep a $100 bill when you use a hotel swimming pool?

Why is it important to keep balcony doors or doors to neighboring rooms locked?

Chapter
Overview

Chapter
Overview

Knowing some of the language of the place or places you will travel to is helpful.

Learning about the culture of a country before you visit is a good idea.

Unfamiliar money can pose a challenge to travelers.

Most foreign countries require citizens of other countries to have a passport for entry. Some countries also require a visa.

Chapter **6**

Foreign Travel

This chapter looks at important safety considerations for visiting places with cultures unfamiliar to you. When visiting foreign countries, it is important to become familiar with your destination before travel.

TOR AND LLOYD, AGE 19

Lloyd had spent a great year as a high school exchange student in Nairobi, Kenya. Now he wanted to spend the summer traveling around South Africa. On the train south, he met a Swedish student named Tor. They agreed to travel together and saw a lot of South Africa. Together, they felt safe going to many places that neither might have visited alone. It was a terrific summer. Tor and Lloyd hoped to keep in touch.

When visiting a foreign country, travelers should try to wear clothing that doesn't stand out. They should avoid wearing expensive-looking jewelry. Some criminals target travelers. Plain clothing makes a traveler look less like a tourist.

Travelers to foreign countries can have wonderful adventures. However, the early stages of those adventures can be difficult. For instance, many overseas fliers have jet lag. Time changes throw off their sleep schedule. Sometimes travelers have motion sickness or reactions to new foods. Most of these conditions are temporary. Being in control of more important factors can lessen the effects of these minor ones.

Different Languages

Even a little knowledge of the native language can help you feel more in control during your trip. Unless you have studied the language of your destination country, you should get a phrase book. This can help you with things you want to say and read as a traveler. Even if you know some of the language, a phrase book still may be helpful. Another idea is to practice the language by listening to it on audiocassettes. Libraries and bookstores usually have these available.

Different Customs

It is important to learn about customs that differ from those in Canada and the United States. For instance, some countries hold religious or holiday festivals and celebrations different from yours. Such events can affect travel plans. In some countries, food may be a problem for people with allergies. In some foreign countries, it is not common to purify tap water. In these places, it is wise to drink only bottled water, juices, or soft drinks.

Getting Around

Learn about your destination's public transportation systems in advance. It's helpful to know how you can get from one place to another. This can help you to avoid surprises such as getting lost or stranded somewhere remote or dangerous. Travel agents can help acquaint you with the public transportation available at your destination. For instance, if you are traveling to Europe, a travel agent might suggest you get a European Railpass Guide.

Most likely you will make daily trips from your hotel. It is important to know where your hotel is in relation to where you are going. Keep the hotel phone number handy. This may help if you have a question while you're out. Assistance may not be available nearby, but you will still have someone to call. It is a good idea to plan and compare itineraries, or travel plans, with other members of your group. Choose an easy-to-find meeting place for regrouping.

Figuring Out Measurements and Money

Almost all countries in the world use the metric system for weight and measurement. All countries have different currencies, or money, from those used in the United States and Canada. Foreign currency can be confusing for many North American travelers.

The following chart shows how to convert metric measurements to U.S. customary measurements:

Metric and Customary Measurements

If you know:	Multiply by:	To get:
Meters	3.3	Feet
Kilometers	0.6	Miles
Kilograms	2.2	Pounds
Liters	1.06	Quarts
Degrees Celsius	1.8 and then add 32	Degrees Fahrenheit

Money

You probably are used to dollars and cents. When it comes to using baht, tugrik, or kwacha, you may feel confused. For instance, it may be shocking to find that lunch in Rome costs several thousand Italian lire. Yet that may equal only a few dollars.

"When I went to Greece with my cousins, we had a great time. Before we left, I thought my uncle was really uptight. He insisted on keeping copies of all of our passports. We all laughed at him. Then, when my backpack that had my passport in it was stolen, I stopped laughing. It was pretty easy to get a new passport, thanks to my uncle's precaution."
—Rayna, age 16

Learning about converting money before you travel can make keeping track of unfamiliar money easier. You can know what to expect when you go to convert money. If you are traveling to only a few places, getting some currency for each country before travel may be helpful. For a fee, many banks can convert dollars into foreign currency.

Imports and Exports

Before returning to North America from another country, find out what items you can legally bring back. For instance, many countries do not allow unwrapped food products across borders. Never travel with illegal drugs. Many travelers end up in foreign jails because they were caught with illegal drugs. Carry any prescription medicines in their original bottle. Be sure your name is on the label. If a stranger wants you to carry something, say no and report the person to authorities.

Passports, Visas, and Other Important Documents

Most foreign countries require a passport for entry. However, some countries do not require passports for visitors from the United States or Canada. For instance, Canadian citizens traveling to the United States or U.S. citizens traveling to Bermuda do not need a passport. However, proof of citizenship is needed. This is usually a certified birth certificate or certificate of naturalization (if you were not born in the United States). A photo identification card is necessary as well.

Some countries require a certificate of vaccination, or protection, against diseases like yellow fever or cholera. The U.S. Centers for Disease Control and Prevention (CDC) has more information on vaccination requirements. The number is 1-877-FYI-TRIP (877-394-8747).

Travel experts recommend making several photocopies of your passport and other important documents. Leave one copy with someone at home. Carry the other copies with you while you travel. That way, if your passport is lost or stolen, replacing it will be easier.

Some countries require a visa as well as a passport. A visa is permission to enter a specific country and is usually good for only a limited time. For instance, a visa to travel to Algeria is good for a 90-day visit. Chapter 7 describes how to get a passport and visa.

If you have medical problems, you may need photocopies of several documents. For instance, you should have an international health certificate signed by a doctor. You should have a doctor's letter about any prescription medicines. This will prevent problems if customs authorities question whether medicines you have are legal.

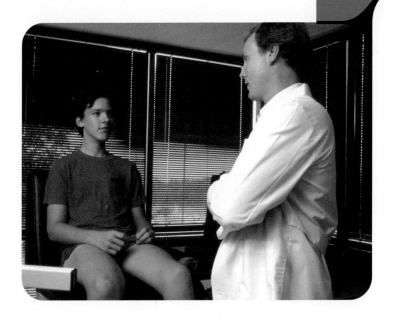

Points to Consider

Imagine you are in a foreign country. How could you tell someone you were ill if you didn't speak the language?

What do you think would be most difficult about traveling to a foreign country?

How could you find out about a country's customs?

Do you think making purchases with unfamiliar currency could be difficult? Why or why not?

Before departing, travelers should find out about the safety of places they will stay.

The U.S. State Department issues consular information sheets for every country in the world.

Travelers need to allow enough time to obtain passports, visas, and other travel documents.

Travelers should make and use a safety checklist while planning their trip.

Chapter **7**

Preparing to Travel

Preparing to Travel Within North America

Many sources of information are available to plan trips within North America. Bookstores, libraries, and local and national governments can provide a wealth of information. Travel clubs, travel agencies, and even car manufacturers offer travelers' information and help. The Internet is a great source for maps, brochures, and up-to-date travel and weather advisories. See the Useful Addresses and Internet Sites section on page 62 for other information sources.

"I had done all this research before I was going to leave. I printed out page after page from the Internet. I read all the brochures that the travel agent had sent. The day before my flight was scheduled to leave, I heard a story on the news. It was about a political event that had just occurred in the country I was traveling to. I was worried. My dad and I got on the Internet and checked out the U.S. State Department's site. It gave more information about what had happened. It said travel was still safe. Both my dad and I were relieved."

LETITIA, AGE 17

Preparing to Travel in Other Countries

You already know that becoming familiar with your destination can make travel safer and more carefree. You may wonder what to do about unexpected events. For example, you do the recommended research and reading on your travel destination. Then shortly before it is time for you to leave, you read an article in the newspaper. It mentions something about a political problem, food safety, or a drop in the currency exchange rate.

Some countries do not allow people to take photographs of particular areas of the country. For example, some police, military, or government buildings and transportation facilities may be off limits. Authorities may hold or question people who photograph such things. Authorities may keep cameras or film, too.

Such news may make you feel uneasy. Events or changes such as these were not mentioned in the brochures or travel books. Before leaving for the airport, you may want to get your questions answered. One of the most effective places to get up-to-date information is the U.S. State Department.

Travel Warnings and Consular Information

Sometimes governments recommend that their citizens not travel to certain foreign countries. This sort of statement is called a travel warning. It is usually made because of political problems within the country.

Most countries you visit do not have a travel warning from the U.S. government. Still, a good source of information is the U.S. State Department. It issues consular information sheets on travel to every country in the world. These sheets include the location and emergency phone numbers for the U.S. embassy or consulates in the country. A consulate is an agency that protects the citizens of one country while they are in another country.

These sheets also will describe unusual health conditions and political disturbances. Other subjects include unusual currency and entry regulations, crime and security information, and drug penalties.

Getting Passports, Visas, and Other Documents

To get a passport, fill out an application and send the Passport Office a birth certificate or a certificate of naturalization. You supply two identical face-shot photos of yourself and a fee of $65. You may need to give proof of immunization, or protection against disease, signed by a doctor. Unless you personally visit the Passport Office, allow up to two months for processing once you mail your application. Check with the office for ways to speed up the process if you need a passport sooner.

Some Middle Eastern or African countries do not issue visas or allow entry if a person's passport shows travel to Israel. If you think this might interfere with your travel plans, call the National Passport Information Center at 1-888-498-3648.

The embassy of the country you are planning to visit will provide you with a visa. For example, to travel to Cambodia, you would get a visa from the Cambodian Embassy. The processing requirements are similar to those for a passport. A visa can take a long time to process, depending on the particular country you intend to visit.

Part of planning ahead may include finding out about requirements for driving in another country. For instance, in some countries you must have an international driver's license. If you are an American driving to Canada, you need a nonresident interprovincial motor vehicle liability insurance card. Contact your insurance agent to get one. This proves that you are covered by the minimum vehicle insurance that Canadian law requires.

A Travel Planning Checklist

Use the following list as a quick safety reference as you prepare to travel.

- ❏ I have a money belt for my valuables.

- ❏ I have luggage that is easy to transport.

- ❏ I have collected and reviewed maps of and information about my destination.

- ❏ I know about the customs of my destination.

- ❏ I have received my passport and visa.

- ❏ I have photocopies of important travel documents.

- ❏ I have read consular information sheets about my destination.

- ❏ I am confident that I am staying in safe places.

- ❏ I have arranged for driving at my destination.

- ❏ I have discussed my safety concerns with my travel agent.

- ❏ I have medicines such as headache or diarrhea remedies.

- ❏ I have left unnecessary or conspicuous clothing or expensive-looking jewelry at home.

- ❏ I have a flashlight with fresh batteries.

- ❏ I have an assortment of bandages and antibiotic ointment.

- ❏ I have a prepaid calling card from a major long-distance telephone company.

- ❏ I have a list of people who can be contacted at home.

- ❏ I have a battery-operated alarm clock.

- ❏ I have an extra copy of my travel itinerary, including ticket numbers.

- ❏ I have an extra copy of my driver's license and insurance information.

- ❏ I have a list of medicines, prescriptions, allergies, and doctors' phone numbers.

- ❏ I have stored my cash away from my wallet or purse.

You can get news about foreign countries at these numbers:

U.S. State Department Office of American Citizen Services: 1-202-647-5225 (not a toll-free call)

Centers for Disease Control 24-hour International Travelers' Hot Line: 1-888-232-3228

The State Department also has an Internet site:

www.travel.state.gov

Points to Consider

Whom can Americans contact for information or assistance about travel in a particular country? Whom can Canadians contact?

What travel advice would you give a friend who is planning travel to a foreign country?

Why do you think the U.S. State Department offers travel warnings?

How much time do you think it takes to prepare for a trip to a foreign country?

What three reminder questions would you add to the travel planning checklist?

Glossary

ambassador (am-BASS-uh-dur)—an official representative of a country; the ambassador lives in the foreign country.

consulate (KON-suh-luht)—an agency that the government of one country sets up in another to protect its citizens

currency (KUR-uhn-see)—the form of money used in a country

dead bolt (DED bohlt)—type of strong, secure lock

deboard (dee-BORD)—to get off a form of transportation

departure (di-PAR-chur)—the act of leaving to go on a journey

destination (dess-tuh-NAY-shuhn)—the place that a person or vehicle is traveling to

embassy (EM-buh-see)—the official place in a foreign country where an ambassador lives and works

hub (HUHB)—a center of activity

immunization (im-yuh-nuh-ZAY-shuhn)—a medicine to prevent someone from getting a disease

itinerary (eye-TIN-uh-rer-ee)—a detailed plan for a journey

jet lag (JET LAG)—a feeling of tiredness or confusion after a plane flight from a different time zone

passport (PASS-port)—an official booklet that proves you are a citizen of a certain country and allows you to travel abroad

traveler's check (TRAV-uh-lurz CHEK)—a draft purchased from a bank that the purchaser signs immediately and signs again when cashing; only the purchaser may use the check.

visa (VEE-zuh)—a document that gives a person permission to enter a specific foreign country at a particular time

For More Information

Chaiet, Donna. *Staying Safe While Traveling.* New York: Rosen, 1995.

Gedatus, Gus. *Violence in Public Places.* Mankato, MN: Capstone, 2000.

Rafkin, Louise. *Street Smarts: A Personal Safety Guide for Women.* San Francisco: HarperCollins, 1995.

Useful Addresses and Internet Sites

Division of Quarantine
National Center for Infectious Diseases
Centers for Disease Control and Prevention
1600 Clifton Road
Atlanta, GA 30333
International Traveler's Hotline 1-888-232-3228
Travelers' Health Section at
www.cdc.gov/travel

National Organization for Victim Assistance
1757 Park Road Northwest
Washington, DC 20010
www.try-nova.org

U.S. State Department
Bureau of Consular Affairs
2201 C Street Northwest
Washington, DC 20520
http://travel.state.gov/passport_services.html
http://travel.state.gov/travel_warnings.html

American Automobile Association (AAA)
www.aaa.com
Travel information by location

Fodor's Resource Center
www.fodors.com/resource
Information about travel issues in different
areas of the world, with a link to a currency
converter

MapQuest
www.mapquest.com
Maps and directions for North America and
Great Britain

Rick Steves' 2000 Guide to European Railpass
www.ricksteves.com/rail
Information on Eurail Passes, Europass,
schedules, and more

Safe Within
www.safewithin.com/travelsafe
Travel safety tips on both domestic and
international travel

TravelCanada
www.travelcanada.ca/travelcanada/index.cfm
Information on Canadian destinations, places
to stay, restaurants, and weather conditions

Index

Index continued